# THE WARRIOR'S ROAD

# LINKA
## THE SKY
# CONQUEROR

*With special thanks to Tabitha Jones*

*For Helen, Isobel and Joe*

www.beastquest.co.uk

ORCHARD BOOKS
338 Euston Road, London NW1 3BH
*Orchard Books Australia*
Level 17/207 Kent St, Sydney, NSW 2000

A Paperback Original
First published in Great Britain in 2013

Beast Quest is a registered trademark of Beast Quest Limited
Series created by Beast Quest Limited, London

Text © Beast Quest Limited 2013
Inside illustrations by Pulsar Estudio (Beehive Illustration)
Cover illustration by Steve Sims © Orchard Books 2013

A CIP catalogue record for this book is available from
the British Library.

ISBN 978 1 40832 405 9

1 3 5 7 9 10 8 6 4 2

Printed in Great Britain by CPI Group (UK) Ltd, Croydon, CR0 4YY

Orchard Books is a division of Hachette Children's Books,
an Hachette UK company

www.hachette.co.uk

# LINKA
## THE SKY
## CONQUEROR

## BY ADAM BLADE

ORCHARD

ICY MOUNTAIN REGION

ERRINEL

Greetings, whoever reads this.

I am Tanner, Avantia's first Master of the Beasts. I fear I have little time left. My life slips away, and I write these few words as a testament for whoever may come across my remains. I have reached the end of my final journey. But a new warrior's journey is just beginning...

With the death of a Master, a new hero must take on the responsibility of guarding the kingdom of Avantia. Avantia needs a true warrior to wear the Golden Armour. He or she must walk the Warrior's Road – a test of valour and strength. I have succeeded, but it has cost me my life. I only hope those who follow survive.

May fortune be with you,

Tanner

# PROLOGUE

Aldo gritted his teeth. His arms were burning. Beneath him, the rock face plunged away to meet the dusty scrub far below. He could feel his muscles cramping. Aldo gripped the rock tightly with one hand, then let go with the other, shaking it to get rid of the pain.

*Slap!* His hand was back on the rock, just before his other arm gave way.

*Phew! That was close.*

Aldo shook out his other hand, then quickly wiped the sweat from his eyes.

All about him, the sky stretched away, a deep unwavering blue. The mountains of his home shone in the morning sun. Aldo grinned. He ached all over, but the view made the climb worth it.

*Even without the money...*

Aldo bent to untie the rope from the spiked peg his sister had left in the rock face.

"Come on!" Asha called. Aldo felt the rope tighten about his waist as his sister took up the slack from the peg. He shielded his eyes, and squinted up at her. She was craning her neck to look down at him.

"Be careful!" Aldo called. "I'm not giving up because you have an accident. If that lady's willing to pay good money for Stoneglass, I mean to get her some."

"Well, come on then! By the time we reach the top, any Stoneglass left will have grown legs and walked away!"

Aldo shrugged his backpack higher and turned back to the climb. Asha was always in such a hurry. She hadn't even wanted to use ropes, but their father had made them promise. Aldo and Asha had been climbing since they could walk, but Sunspear was dangerous, even for them. No one climbed Sunspear any more. And they'd have to reach the top if they expected to find any Stoneglass. The lower reaches had been picked clean long ago.

Aldo reached up as far as he could and dug his fingers into a crack in the stone. The muscles in his legs bunched and his arms strained as he pushed himself higher.

He clung to the cliff for a moment, considering his next step. A huge fissure gaped in the rock face above him. Aldo dried each hand in turn on his tunic and heaved himself into the long, narrow crack.

*WHOOSH!*

A gust of wind nearly ripped Aldo from the rock. He grabbed for the walls of the crack as a cold shadow swept over him. He turned…

…and gasped. His blood ran icy cold. A vast winged shape was swooping towards him, blocking out the sun. It looked something like an eagle, but it was far too big. Aldo staggered back, battered by the wind from the creature's mighty wings. It was coming right for him! The great bird dipped its head and a huge orange eye peered into the crack.

Aldo shrank against the rock,
wedging himself deep into the furthest
reaches of the fissure. He clenched his

teeth, waiting for the stab of needle claws...but no! The bird didn't have claws. It didn't even have legs! It had a long scaly tail tipped with a gleaming, bulbous sting.

*Keeeaaaah!* The bird screeched – a terrible, grating shriek. Its tail lashed towards Aldo. He screamed and flung up his arms just as the glistening point jerked to a stop, a hand's breadth from his face. The tail whipped away, then stabbed again, almost brushing Aldo's tunic. Aldo felt a flicker of hope. *Its tail isn't long enough to reach me!*

The bird shook its wings and screamed, ripping at the rock face with its beak. Aldo heard the clatter of falling stones. The edges of the crack were beginning to crumble! He pushed himself hard against the rock as the bird thrust its head towards him, its sharp beak gaping wide.

Then it was gone and sunlight filled the fissure. Aldo drew a shuddering breath of relief. The bird was swooping upwards and away.

A fresh wave of terror crashed over him. *Asha*. Aldo scrambled to the edge of the crack and craned his neck upwards.

"Asha!" Aldo called.

"*Aaaaah!*" Asha's scream filled Aldo with horror. All he could see above him was flapping wings and tawny feathers. A length of rope fell towards him, snaking through the air.

Aldo's throat tightened. His body went numb.

It was the rope that had bound him to his sister.

# CHAPTER ONE

# A VICIOUS FOE

Tom strained against the hands that gripped his tunic, trying to twist himself free, but the Hooded Man was just too strong. Silver snarled.

"Tom! No!" Elenna cried. But there was nothing Tom could do. Finally, he let himself fall forwards, through the door in the side of the tree.

Darkness met him, and sudden silence. The sounds of the jungle were gone, and the only light was from the smouldering red embers of a dying fire. Tom could just make out the craggy walls of a cavern far above him. He stared into the dark, straining his eyes.

The man stood a few paces away, an inky blot in the darkness. He was leaning against the wall of the cave, his bearded face shrouded in shadow and his eyes glittering coldly. An icy finger seemed to trace Tom's spine as he met the stranger's gaze.

Tom drew his sword. The rasp of steel echoed through the cavern. "Who are you?" Tom asked.

There was an answering hiss as the shadowy figure drew his own blade. "Who am I?" he sneered. "You should know that better than anyone." His sword shone in the firelight. "Now! It's time to see how your sword-fighting is

faring." The stranger lunged.

*Ching!* Tom parried the blow almost
before he saw it. The shock of it jolted
along his arm. The man swung again,
his blade slicing for Tom's face.

*Clang!* Sparks flew as Tom smashed
the blow aside. He felt his pulse

quicken, his mind grow sharp.

The stranger jabbed and lunged, a blur of shadows and red-tinged steel. Each time the Hooded Man struck, Tom's blade was ready, but the man was forcing him backwards. Tom shifted his balance, trying to keep his weight off his injured foot. He watched the stranger's movements, feeling for their rhythm...

Tom spun away, dodging his enemy's slicing blade. He called on all his strength and sent his own sword swooping towards the man in a double-handed blow. It should have been enough. It should have sent his opponent reeling, but the cloaked figure just batted Tom's sword aside.

Tom stumbled, his bad ankle buckling under him. He managed to keep his balance, blocking a vicious slice from above. Then another, and another. Tom's breath was rasping in his throat. His heart beat hard, but his opponent showed no sign of slowing. *I will not let you beat me!*

From the corner of his eye, Tom caught a flare of gold. He glanced towards it and saw a pair of shadows. Elenna and Silver.

"Stay back!" Tom cried, as deadly steel sliced towards him.

Tom raised his sword. The stranger's blow rang away in a shower of sparks, but Tom could feel his muscles tiring, his movements growing slow. He stepped back, holding up his blade.

"Why do you fight me?" Tom said. "I mean you no harm."

The Hooded Man stopped. His eyes narrowed to angry slits. "Quiet, boy!" he snapped. "Save your breath for the fight. Or better still, give up." Tom stared into the shadows, trying to make out the man's face, but all he could see was the glitter of deep-set eyes in the firelight. "Turn back and I might let you live," the man said.

Anger gripped Tom. "Never!"

He swung his sword in a sideways arc. The man dodged and spun around to make his own attack, but Tom was ready. He parried and struck back fast and hard. The two swords clashed together. The Hooded Man stumbled, his boots scuffling in the embers of the dying fire. Tom was after him in a second. Brittle coals crunched beneath his boots, sending up clouds of ash.

Tom lifted his sword and struck again. His eyes burned from the stinging ash and his ankle screamed with pain, but he was driving his

opponent back, step by step towards
the wall. Finally, there was nowhere
to go. The Hooded Man was cornered.

"Why are you doing this?" said Tom.

"If you think you can walk the
Warrior's Road, you're more stupid

than I thought," said his enemy.

The words hit Tom like a slap. He drew himself up and glared into the eyes beneath the hood. "What do you know of my Quest?" he asked.

The man laughed. It was a bitter sound. "I know more than an ignorant pup like you will ever learn," he growled. "More than you could imagine. The Road isn't for children. It's not even for most men."

A swell of rage started deep in the pit of Tom's belly. What could this man know of the Road? The Evil Judge, leader of the Circle of Wizards, had sent Tom to walk Tanner's final journey. Until he did, he couldn't call himself Master of the Beasts and Avantia would be without a protector. Tom was the first to tread the Road in generations.

"Go back to making horseshoes and

pretty trinkets in your uncle's forge,"
said the Hooded Man. "You might just
be good enough for that...if the post of
village idiot isn't already taken."

"*Gah!*" Tom swung his sword down
towards the stranger's chest. The man
flitted out of reach like a shadow.

*Clang!* Tom's sword struck the wall.
He tried to draw it back, but it was
stuck. Tom heaved, bracing his feet
on the floor. He could feel the man
watching him, getting ready to strike.

The stranger pounced like a cat. His
boot crashed towards Tom's arm.

*Smash!* Pain exploded through Tom's
fingers.

He gritted his teeth and turned to
meet the stranger's icy gaze. Tom
swallowed his fear and lifted his chin,
waiting for the final, mortal blow.

# CHAPTER TWO

# A CRY FOR HELP

Time almost seemed to stop.
Everything was slow and bright and
clear. Tom watched as the silver blade
flashed towards him, cutting a smooth
arc through the shadows.

Suddenly the blade faltered, and
dropped. The stranger gave a cry and
put his hand to his side. An arrow
jutted from his cloak.

*Elenna!* Tom darted into the shadows

after his sword, taking advantage of the Hooded Man's distraction. He'd heard the telltale chink of armour, and knew that his enemy would only have been winded by Elenna's attack.

*I don't have much time*, he thought.

Tom scanned the cavern floor. From the corner of his eye he caught a shimmer of red as the stranger raised his blade. Elenna took a step forward, her bow aimed and ready.

"I'd stop there if I were you," she said. "My next arrow will bury itself in your skull. Disarm or die."

Tom thought he heard a low chuckle as the Hooded Man lowered his blade then strode towards the cave mouth.

"Disarm!" Elenna said. "That was your final warning."

As the man turned towards Elenna, Tom caught a glimpse of his face in

the light from outside the cave. The
man was well past middle age, and
scarred. His bearded face was as gnarled
and lined as ancient oak. There was
something about his eyes though...
something familiar.

"You won't fire," the man said,
driving his sword back into its scabbard.

Elenna glared at him down her arrow. The man tipped back his head and laughed. He lifted his hands. "See? I know you too well. You're weak. You'd never kill a man at your mercy." The man turned his back again and strode from the cave.

"*Grrrr!*" Elenna lowered her bow.

Tom went to retrieve his sword. He was shaking with fury.

"What was that all about?" Elenna asked.

"I don't know," Tom said. "But I've never met a better swordsman. Or a more vicious one." He walked to the narrow mouth of the cave and stopped. The ground fell away at his feet to meet a rock-strewn path below. In every direction, as far as Tom could see, barren peaks climbed into a blazing sky.

Tom squinted down the rocky

trail below the cave. The man was nowhere to be seen, but Tom could just make out the shifting, winding red path of the Warrior's Road – the path that was visible only to him. He tilted his head to get a better view, but the path flickered and faded in the heat.

*If only I still had Daltec's map!*

Tom turned back into the cave, Elenna and Silver close behind him.

"What is this place?" Elenna said, peering out at the horizon.

"I'm not sure," Tom said, "but I do know that man was trying to kill me. He would have done too, if it hadn't been for your quick thinking." Tom met Elenna's eyes. "Thank you."

Elenna smiled. "All in a day's work," she said. She glanced down at Silver. His ears were pricked and twitching. "He's heard something," Elenna said.

Tom listened. A thin wail drifted across the rocky terrain. A cry for help.

"Quick!" Tom seized his sword. "Our enemy may have found a new victim."

Tom and Elenna scrambled down onto the rocky path. It was steep and crooked, and treacherous with shifting rubble. Tom winced each time a loose rock moved under his feet.

Silver padded ahead, weaving between rocky outcrops with his nose close to the ground. Sometimes he lifted his muzzle and sniffed the air, then turned back to the path to lead Tom and Elenna onwards.

Finally, Silver stopped in the shadow of a towering cliff. There was some sort of bundle at his feet, and he dipped his nose to nudge it. A slim brown hand reached towards him.

"Silver, to me!" Elenna called. She

hurried to the rock face. Tom dashed to her side, ignoring the pain in his ankle.

A girl was lying slumped, her leg twisted awkwardly. Her clothes were in tatters and a frayed rope was tied about her waist. The girl gazed up, her eyes glassy. "Please," she whimpered. "Please, Aldo...I'm so thirsty."

*Who's Aldo?* Tom wondered. *And are we too late to help this girl?*

# CHAPTER THREE

# TERROR IN THE MOUNTAINS

"Here, sip this," Tom said, putting his flask to the injured girl's lips.

She spluttered and coughed, her eyes rolling back as she drank.

"Not too much just yet, or you'll be sick," Elenna said, easing the girl back down. "Can you tell us what happened?"

The girl blinked up at them. "Aldo!"

she moaned. "My brother. He's gone. The eagle... It was so big. Too big, and it had no legs..."

Tom and Elenna exchanged a puzzled glance as the girl went on.

"We couldn't get the Stoneglass," the girl said, "we couldn't get down. We..." The girl glanced at the sky, her eyes wide with terror. "Aldo!" she cried. "Aldo!"

The girl squeezed her eyes shut. Her face twisted, then went slack.

"She's fainted," Elenna said. She placed her hand on the girl's forehead. "If she doesn't get help soon, she could die. Tom, do you think she met our next Beast?"

"Maybe," Tom said. "I'm not sure, though. An eagle without legs? It doesn't make sense. It would never be able to land. She's delirious." Tom sighed and thought for a moment. *We should be following the Warrior's Road... but we can't leave the girl.* "There's nothing more we can do here," Tom said. "We don't know where this girl's brother is, or if he's even alive. Let's take her and follow the path. She must live somewhere nearby, or she would have been carrying water."

He slipped his arms under the girl's shoulders and Elenna cradled her legs. "Ready?" Tom said. Elenna nodded, and they both lifted.

As soon as Tom put weight on his damaged ankle, a sickening pain shot up his leg. He gritted his teeth and swallowed.

They started off slowly, easing their burden through narrow gaps and around jagged outcrops until they reached the track. Even then, progress was slow. Tom's ankle throbbed with every step. The girl whimpered and twisted. A gritty wind scoured the mountain path, throwing dust into their faces.

Tom almost thought he could hear the keening of an eagle on the wind, or sometimes a cry for help. He thought of the girl's missing brother. But even if Aldo was out there, they couldn't leave the girl. She would die.

"It can't be much further," Elenna said, shifting the girl's weight in her arms. "Look!"

Tom squinted into the wind. Silver was sitting beside a standing stone just before a bend in the road. He lifted his nose and howled.

"He's found something," Elenna said.

Silver waited for them to catch up, then trotted around the bend.

Tom and Elenna followed him into a sheltered valley. A cluster of stone huts was spread across the valley floor, and goats grazed the dusty scrub around the buildings. The path dipped sharply down to run through the little town.

"This must be where our girl lives," Tom said.

They carried the helpless girl down towards the centre of the village, goats shying away from them as they passed.

Somewhere nearby, a bell began to ring.

One by one, men and women emerged from the huts. Some carried spears. They watched silently as Tom and Elenna approached, glancing warily at Silver, and at the injured girl.

A tanned, weather-beaten man with gnarled skin stepped away from the group and strode towards Tom and Elenna. *He must be their leader*, thought Tom. The man's eyes widened as they rested on the girl, then he turned towards a tall woman by the huts.

"Denka," he said. "Take Asha to Seren."

The woman strode towards Tom and Elenna, beckoning for a boy to join her. The two of them eased Asha from Tom and Elenna's arms. Tom watched as the girl was hurried away.

"She'll be all right," Elenna said, following Tom's gaze.

After Denka had disappeared into the village, the man nodded to Tom. "Welcome to Pyrus. I am Oran. We have been expecting you."

Tom felt a flicker of unease. "Expecting us?" he said.

He smiled. "Your princess arrived before you. I will take you to her now."

Elenna turned to Tom and raised an eyebrow. "Our princess?" she mouthed.

Tom shrugged. *King Hugo has no daughter. Something very odd is going on...*

# CHAPTER FOUR

# A PERILOUS BARGAIN

"Come!" Oran said. Tom, Elenna and Silver followed him towards a low, circular hut at the heart of the village.

A thick tapestry hung in the doorway to the hut, and sweet-smelling smoke drifted out onto the breeze.

Oran extended his arm towards the doorway. "Your princess," he said.

Tom lifted the tapestry and stepped inside. The hut was nothing like he'd expected. The dusky space was lined from wall to wall with embroidered cushions and patterned rugs dyed in rich, earthy tones.

In the centre of the room, on a low wooden couch covered with cushions and throws, lay a girl in a deep-blue robe. Tom felt a shock of recognition. Beside him, Elenna drew a sharp breath. He knew the girl only too well, and she was definitely no princess. She'd once been apprentice to the Evil Wizard Malvel, but now she was a Witch in her own right.

"Petra!" said Tom.

Their old enemy yawned. She took a grape from a plate at her side and ate it slowly. When she finally lifted her eyes to Tom, they were sparkling and

full of mischief. "You took your time,"
she said.

Tom folded his arms. He didn't
know whether to be more annoyed or
relieved. Petra was trouble, no doubt
about it, but she did know a thing or

two about magic. She might just be able to get them back on the Warrior's Road. "What are you doing here?" he asked. "And how did you know we were coming?"

Petra inspected her fingernails. "Oh, it's common knowledge among those of us with power that you're on a mission doomed to failure." Her eyes flicked back to Tom's. "You do know your Quest is impossible?"

Tom gritted his teeth. "While there's blood in my veins, I'll walk the Warrior's Road," he said.

Petra rolled her eyes and turned to Elenna. "How do you put up with him?" she asked. "Blood in my veins this, conquer that. So heroic." Tom saw Elenna scowl, but Petra didn't seem to notice. She sighed softly. "But I didn't come all this way just to watch you two march off to your doom. I'm here for Stoneglass. This is the only place it can still be found. I've sent a couple of climbers to fetch me some."

"Then you'll be disappointed," Tom said. "One of your climbers is missing, and the other is badly injured. We found her in the mountains. She was almost killed following your orders." Tom felt his anger building as he thought of poor Asha. "And what right have you to call yourself the princess of Avantia?"

Petra's cheeks flushed red. "I didn't order them to go up," she said, "I offered to pay, that's all. And it's not my fault they assumed I was royalty just because I showed them a few magic tricks." Petra took another grape from the plate beside her, and popped it into her mouth. "Anyway, what's wrong with wanting to be treated properly? It's about time I was shown some respect."

Elenna sighed. "You're lying to these people. You might not have noticed, but they don't exactly have much."

Petra shrugged. "I am afraid I don't see your point."

"You wouldn't," Elenna said.

"What do you want Stoneglass for, anyway?" Tom asked.

"I'm not going to explain myself to you," Petra said.

Tom felt his anger flare. "You can at least explain why you sent someone to attack us."

Petra looked blank.

"A Hooded Man with a sword?" Elenna said.

Petra tapped her lip in thought. "Nothing to do with me," she said.

"And I can't imagine why anyone else would try to kill you when you're doing such a fine job by yourselves." She waved a hand towards the door. "Don't let me keep you from your Quest. The Warrior's Road isn't going to walk itself. I wish you luck." Petra gave a laugh. "You're definitely going to need it."

Tom took a deep breath. "Actually," he said, "we need more than luck just now. We need your help. We don't know where to rejoin the Road."

Petra lifted her head from her pillows. A smile twitched at the corners of her mouth. "I suppose I could help you find the Road," she said. "But I would need something in return. Hmm...let me think... It would have to be something I can't get anywhere else..." Petra turned her cheek towards

49

him, and brushed a greasy lock of hair aside. "A kiss would do," she said.

Tom felt a jolt of disgust. *Kiss Petra? Urgh!* He hesitated for a moment, trying not to grimace, then started slowly towards her.

Petra gaped, then burst into laughter. "You were actually going to do it, weren't you?" She laughed so hard it was all Tom could do to stop himself storming from the hut. "No," Petra said. "What I need is Stoneglass. Bring me some Stoneglass, and I'll show you your Road."

Tom glanced at Elenna. He could see that she didn't trust Petra any more than he did.

"How do we know that you'll keep your side of the bargain?" he asked angrily. "You're hardly known for your honesty."

Petra shrugged. "I don't see that you have much choice. That's my offer. Take it or leave it, I don't much care either way."

Tom sighed. "We'll get you your Stoneglass," he said. "Just tell us where to find it."

Petra smiled. "I suppose you noticed the mountain out there that's twice as high as all the others?"

Tom nodded. It was the mountain where they'd found Asha.

"It's called Sunspear. The only Stoneglass left can be found right at the very top. But for seasoned heroes like you, I guess that shouldn't be too much trouble."

Tom felt his mouth turn dry. His ankle started to throb at just the thought of the climb.

"No trouble at all," he said.

# CHAPTER FIVE

# CLIMBING SUNSPEAR

"Here, you'll need these." Oran
handed Tom a coil of rope, then
passed a clinking bag to Elenna, who
drew out a handful of spiked pegs.

"Thank you," she said. "These may
save our lives."

"Once you're at the top," Oran said
gruffly, "the Stoneglass won't be hard
to find. There should be some at the

surface. It used to be found all over, but most was taken long ago, before we could trade for steel."

"What does Stoneglass look like?" Elenna asked.

"You'll know it if you see it. It's black, yet it shines."

Elenna turned to Tom. "I have a bad feeling about this," she said. "You shouldn't be walking on that ankle, let alone climbing. And shiny rock? I hope we're not risking our necks so that Petra can make a necklace."

Tom looked down at his newly bound ankle, ignoring the slightly foul smell from the poultice of herbs the village healer had applied. It was already feeling much better, and the healer had said it would be as good as new – but only if Tom made sure to get some rest...

*There isn't much of that on a Beast Quest*, Tom thought ruefully.

"I can't help worrying that Petra's got something more evil in mind than jewellery," he said. "Still, we don't have any choice. We have to get back on the Road. And that boy, Aldo. He might be trapped up there. We can't just leave him to die."

"You're right." Elenna sighed.
"I suppose we'd better go now."

They stepped outside the hut to find
Petra waiting.

"Going already?" Petra said. "Such
enthusiasm!" Her eyes glittered.
"I suppose I ought to tell you though,
you might run into a Beast. Her
name's Linka the Sky Conqueror. She
terrorises these mountains whenever
someone tries to walk the Road." Petra
grinned. "Try not to die. I really need
that Stoneglass."

Tom didn't smile. "I'll do my best,"
he said.

"Perfect! Then I'll leave you to it."
Petra turned and hurried back towards
her hut.

Elenna glared after her. "I don't trust
that girl," she said. Silver growled in

agreement. "What if the Judge sent her to sabotage our Quest? I'm sure he'd stoop to anything to make sure we fail."

"Then we'd better keep an eye out for traps," Tom said.

Elenna nodded. "And Silver can help keep watch for Linka. Although I'm hoping we don't run into her up there."

Tom let his breath out slowly. 'If we do, we do. We have to face her some time."

Tom, Elenna and Silver set off through the quiet town. The sun was blazing high in the sky and the shadows had all but disappeared as they passed the last of the huts.

"Wait!" a girl's voice called out.

Tom turned to find Asha hobbling towards them on a pair of home-made crutches.

"Asha!" Elenna cried. "Are you all right?"

Asha's face was pale and her eyes were wide. "You saved my life,"

she said. "I'm so grateful. But that monster..." Asha shuddered. "I'm afraid that it got Aldo." Tears started to run down her cheeks. "I'm sorry," she said. "But I miss him so much. Please. There must be a chance—"

Tom stopped her with his hand. "We'll find your brother," he said. "I promise."

"Thank you!" Asha looked as if she might say something more, but then turned and hobbled away, still sobbing quietly.

Elenna looked grave. "I hope you're right," she said.

Tom sighed. "We'll find him," he said. "I just hope we find him alive."

Tom, Elenna and Silver walked in silence, following the steep trail that led back to Sunspear.

As they approached the mountain's

rocky base, Tom shaded his eyes and looked up at the craggy peak. The higher he looked, the steeper the rock became. Much of the climb would be almost sheer.

Silver whimpered, and Elenna bent to ruffle his fur. "Goodbye," Elenna said. "Wait here and watch for trouble. We should be back before sundown." Silver licked her face, then settled back on his haunches.

Tom and Elenna started slowly through the boulders and rocks that covered the base of the peak. Before long, the mountainside began to slope upwards.

"Time to start climbing," Tom said. He shrugged the coil of rope from his shoulder.

"I'll go first," Elenna said. "You hold the rope." Tom didn't argue. He was going to have to take it slowly, with his ankle so badly injured. They each tied one end of the rope about their waists, then Elenna shoved her toe into a crack in the rock, and pushed herself upwards.

Tom passed the rope though his hands as Elenna climbed. Elenna hammered spiked pegs into the rock and attached their rope as she went, so even if she fell she wouldn't go far. When Tom climbed up after her, he would remove the pegs and Elenna would reel in the rope.

Tom was amazed at how quickly Elenna climbed. Before long, the rope was all paid out. Elenna secured herself to the rock face, and turned back to Tom.

"I've got you," she called. Tom reached as high as he could, and pulled himself upwards, feeling for a foothold with his good leg. There was a narrow ledge in the rock...

Tom pressed his toes onto the ledge and pushed up, then reached up with his other foot. As soon as he rested his weight on it, pain shot up his leg.

He gritted his teeth, and pulled

himself up with his arms, using his bad foot just for balance. He could already feel the strain he was placing on his muscles. *This is not going to be easy...*

When Tom finally made it to the narrow shelf where Elenna waited, he was exhausted, and his arms were burning. Elenna handed him a flask of water.

"Thanks!" Tom took the flask with shaking hands, and drank.

Once his arms had recovered, he gripped the rope with both hands, and Elenna started to climb.

All through the morning they took it in turns to scale the mountain. Tom was thankful for the rests this gave him. His ankle throbbed and his arms felt stiff from the extra work.

It was windy too, now they were

higher. Gusts came at Tom from every direction as he heaved himself up the rock. They lashed at his hair and tunic, and seemed to rip the air right out of his lungs.

Tom reached as high as he could, gasping for breath as he strained to reach the next hold. *I can do this!* he told himself. After all, what choice did he have? If he failed in this Quest, Avantia would be without a Master of the Beasts – and it would be under the Judge's control.

A long, urgent howl cut through Tom's train of thought. "Silver?"

He heard a brittle, pattering sound, and his heart gave a jolt.

*Rock fall!*

"Elenna, watch out!"

He got a faceful of grit as he looked up. Blinking, he heard his friend scream, then something smashed into his shoulder with a bolt of pain. "Ugh!"

Tom lost his grip on the rock face and his stomach lurched as he tumbled free. Jagged stone rushed past his face as he plummeted to the ground.

# CHAPTER SIX

# PREY OF THE WINGED BEAST

"Oof!" Tom was jerked upwards by the waist.

He dangled in the air, hanging from the rope like a puppet. The cliff face whirled about him.

*Smash!* His back slammed into the mountain. The dusty ground far below seemed to twist and pulse.

Tom closed his eyes and took a

breath to steady his pounding heart.
*I'm not falling. I just have to right myself.*
He opened his eyes and reached
towards the mountainside. He used
the cracks and crevices to lever
himself around, then reached with his
feet to steady himself against the cliff.

Looking up, he saw Elenna clinging to the mountain above. Her cheek was pressed against the rock and her face was pale.

"Are you all right?" Tom shouted.

"Yes," Elenna called. Her voice was shaking. "How about you?"

"Just about," Tom answered. He had a pain in his forehead and a dull ache in his shoulder to add to the pain in his foot. But they'd been lucky. *If the rope hadn't held, or if one of the pegs had failed...* Tom shuddered and pushed the thought away.

"Let's move over a bit," Elenna called, "in case any more rocks come down."

"Good thinking!" Tom edged across the rock and started to pull himself upwards again. The wind whipped about him, howling through the crevices in the rock face. It sounded like a screaming voice.

"Look out!" Elenna cried. Tom glanced upwards to see more jagged lumps of rock tumbling towards him. He shrank against the cliff face as they skittered down, chips of stone bouncing off his back.

"Help! No! Please!" There was a voice on the wind. It was coming from behind an overhang. Tom scrambled through the falling stones towards the sound. He could see Elenna climbing down from her ledge as well.

Suddenly, Elenna froze. Tom heaved himself over a lip of stone, and gaped upwards. A huge winged Beast was hovering in the air, striking again and again at the mountain with its curved, black beak. *Linka!*

The immense bird's tawny wings beat the air, blasting Tom with putrid gusts. Stones and rubble clattered past his face.

Tom's mind reeled as he tried to make sense of the Beast. He couldn't see her legs, but she had a long snaking tail, thick and feathered at the base but scaled and sinewy towards the end. It finished in a bulbous point, like a scorpion's venomous sting.

"Leave me alone!" a thin voice wailed.

"Aldo!" Tom cried. "Linka must have him cornered."

"We'd better do something, quick, or she'll kill him!" Elenna shouted.

Tom's mind raced. How could he fight a flying Beast while clinging to a cliff? *Maybe if I had something to throw...*

He thought of the rocks clattering past, but even if he could catch one, they'd barely touch the giant beast. As he adjusted his footing, he felt his token sack brush against his leg. A picture flashed through his mind. *Slivka's scale!* It might just work, but he'd only have one chance.

Tom rummaged in his sack, feeling for the hard, curved edge of the scale. He drew it out and leaned back from the cliff, hanging by one hand. His arm strained under his weight. It wouldn't hold him for long... Tom drew a breath, took aim and threw.

The scale soared through the air, spinning.

Linka shrieked, a hideous, rasping screech, as the scale bit into her tail, leaving a bloody gash. She wheeled upwards, beating her tremendous

wings. Her orange eyes glinted as she
scanned the rock face.

*Looking for me, are you?* thought Tom.

*Well, I'm ready!*

"Elenna!" he shouted. "Keep climbing. I'll handle Linka while you get the Stoneglass."

"I'm not leaving you to her!" Elenna cried.

"You can't shoot without both hands," Tom called back. "Go! I can't climb quickly anyway. I have to stand and fight."

Elenna looked back at him, her face pinched with worry, then began to climb.

Tom untied the rope from his waist and Elenna set off hand over hand. Tom felt a swell of pride as he watched her go. Her movements were swift and sure, despite the dizzying drop below her. And there was no one to catch her if she fell...

*Keeeaaahhh!* Linka's grating cry

snatched Tom from his thoughts. He turned, and a jolt ran through him as he met her hungry gaze. He could see he was prey, nothing more.

Linka opened her vicious beak to reveal a gaping, scarlet throat. Tom's muscles tensed as Linka screamed again, then dived towards him.

The Hooded Man's words came back to him in a flash.

*The Road isn't for children.*

Was this the end?

# CHAPTER SEVEN

# A DESPERATE CORNER

Tom adjusted his balance as Linka
wheeled towards him. He gripped
the rock as hard as he could with one
hand, then grabbed for his sword.
Linka screamed again, blasting
Tom with the reek of rotting flesh.
Tom held her gaze as he swung his
sword...

*Smack!* The blade smashed against

Linka's pointed beak.

Her tail whipped towards him.

*Thwack!* Tom swiped it aside.

Linka shrieked in rage, her wings
pounding the air.

*She's retreating!*

Tom clawed at the rock, trying to

get a good grip. He forced his fingers and toes further into the cracks, and glanced up. Elenna was already far above, hopefully beyond Linka's notice.

Linka was diving again. Tom braced himself against the wind from her mighty wings and raised his sword. Linka swooped, her tail lashing out in a deadly arc. Its venom-tipped point whipped straight towards Tom's face. Tom threw himself aside, swinging out on the tips of his fingers and the toes of his injured foot. Pain seared through him, snatching the breath from his throat, but somehow he kept his grip.

Linka's lizard-tail crashed into the rock face right where Tom's head had been. She screamed, drawing her tail back for another vicious strike. Tom's fingers burned. His leg was quivering with pain. *I don't think I can do that again…*

Linka gave a furious, agonised shriek as an arrow buried itself deep in her tail.

Another shaft whizzed past her to clatter against the rock.

*Elenna! She's found somewhere she can shoot!*

Linka soared away screeching, her tail lashing from side to side.

Tom heaved himself up the rock face. His breath came fast and shallow as he forced himself to climb. A great fissure carved through the rock above him. It was surrounded by pale gashes where Linka had torn chunks of stone away. Tom gripped the edge of the crack with both hands, and pulled himself up and in. He tumbled forwards into the narrow gap, landing clumsily on his hands and knees.

A pair of dark eyes stared back at him. A boy cowered in the shadows, his face covered in dust and streaked with tears. His clothes were torn and bloodied.

Tom tried to speak, but he didn't have any breath. He swallowed, and tried again. "Aldo?" he asked.

The boy stared, his eyes round with fear. Finally, he nodded.

"We found...your sister... " Tom panted. "She's safe, back in Pyrus."

Aldo's eyes seemed to brighten for a moment. A hint of colour crept into his cheeks. Then his shoulders slumped.

"But what about that thing?" Aldo wailed. "That thing outside?" A shudder ran through his body. "It's trying to eat me!"

Tom felt shame and anger burning through him. *It's my fault that Linka is here!* He drew a deep breath, and squared his shoulders.

"That Beast is my foe," Tom said. "While there's blood in my veins I will defeat her."

Aldo gaped at Tom as if he had lost his mind. He glanced over Tom's shoulder towards the sky where Linka hovered.

"How?" Aldo asked.

A shriek of anger split the air, and Tom gripped his sword-hilt in a sweaty fist. How? He was about to find out.

# CHAPTER EIGHT

# THE JAGGED
# TEETH OF DEATH

Tom glanced about the narrow cave
that protected him and Aldo from the
Beast. In the furthest reaches of the
crevice lay a coil of climbing rope. He
picked it up.

"I'll need to borrow this," Tom said.
He tied two quick knots, then pushed
a loop of rope through the second.
He'd made a lasso!

Tom scrambled back to the mouth of the crevice and peered around the edge. Linka dived past, screaming. Tom felt a twinge of horror as he saw her underbelly. It was smooth and feathered all the way down. She really didn't have legs! And her tail was so long! *It won't be easy to keep out of reach of that sting.*

He turned back to Aldo. "I'm going out."

"Don't leave me!" Aldo cried. "You said you'd help. You said—"

"Aldo." Tom put a hand on Aldo's shoulder. "Have courage. I'm going out there to fight Linka, but I need your help." Tom could see the struggle in Aldo's face as he tried to control his fear.

"You'll have to stand close to the edge," Tom said.

"But she'll come for me!" Aldo cried.

"That's the idea," Tom said. "But don't worry. I'll be waiting."

Aldo searched Tom's face. He swallowed hard, then nodded.

Tom led Aldo towards the edge of the crack. They crouched side by side and watched as Linka screeched and dived. Tom waited until Linka had passed, then climbed quickly from the crevice and started to work his way up the rock face.

He found a slanting ledge in the rock above the crack. It must have been where Elenna had stopped to shoot, but thankfully she was out of danger now, just a dot on the cliff above. Tom climbed onto the ledge and glanced downwards. Aldo was clinging to the lip of the crevice, his fingers white on the stone.

Linka squawked triumphantly and her orange eyes glinted. *She's spotted him!* thought Tom. The Beast tilted her wings and plunged towards the boy. Tom was ready. As Linka dived, Tom swung his lasso, letting it build up speed.

Linka's shadow fell across Aldo. Tom waited. He had to time it just right....

The Beast stretched out her neck, reaching for her prey. Aldo screamed and fell to his knees.

Tom gave one final swing, then let the lasso fly.

The rope arced through the air as Linka's great beak opened to snatch Aldo from the crack. It dropped over her head, and Tom yanked it tight, pulling with every bit of strength he had.

Linka's head jerked upwards with a

panicked *Kah!* and Aldo scrambled
back, away from her thrashing tail.
She surged towards the sky. Tom

braced himself. The rope bit into his hands, and his arms were wrenched above his head. He clung on with all his might. With a jolting rush of speed, he was torn from the cliff face and up into the sky.

Linka climbed higher and higher,

dragging Tom with her through
the air. His boots dangled and his
stomach churned as the mountain
dropped away.

Icy wind snatched at him, numbing
his hands and chilling his blood.

*Keeeyaaah!*

Tom felt the rope suddenly go slack.
His stomach leaped into his throat.
For a terrifying, heart-stopping
moment he was still, suspended in
the sky. Linka had changed direction.
She was diving...

Tom's teeth smacked together and
his spine jerked as the rope snapped
taut again. His arms burned as he
plummeted through the air. Wind
rushed past his ears, bringing with
it the sound of Silver howling far
below.

Linka was falling faster and

faster, swooping towards the jagged mountain peak.

*She's going to smash me against the rock!*

Tom let go of the rope with one hand. He reached up, and grabbed it again, pulling himself upwards. His hands were numb with cold, but somehow he forced them to open and close. His muscles screamed as he climbed the rope, hand over hand, gasping for air as he went. He risked a glance below. The mountain was growing by the second... Tom could see Elenna clinging on near the top, watching him wide-eyed and open-mouthed.

Jagged rock sped towards him.

A terrible wave of dread and defeat crashed over Tom. There was no way that he could climb up as quickly as

Linka could dive.

*Who will stop Linka once I'm gone?* he thought. *Who will defend Avantia?*

# CHAPTER NINE

# TUG OF WAR

"This is not how I die!" Tom cried.
With one last desperate effort, he
summoned all his strength. He forced
away his fear and pain, and heaved
himself up the rope. His arms shook
and his lungs burned. The mountain
surged towards him. He could almost
touch Linka's feathers...

Tom held his breath and waited as
the mountain peak surged towards

him. Just before his body slammed
into the rock, he swung his legs as
high as he could to clear the peak.
The ground rushed past, inches below
his feet, a blur of jagged stone.

*This is going to hurt...*

Tom let go of the rope.

He hit the ground running as Linka
surged away, but he was going much
too fast! Tom threw himself into
a roll, and tumbled over and over
across the rocky ground.

When everything finally stopped spinning, he was lying on his back in the shadow of a boulder. His head was pounding, his hands were raw, and his body felt battered and bruised.

But he was alive.

Linka soared above him, squawking in delight. Tom could see his lasso trailing out after her.

*She must think I'm dead!*

"Tom!" Tom lifted his head to see Elenna hauling herself over the peak.

Linka's shadow fell across her. Tom's stomach clenched. He scrambled to his feet as the massive Beast swooped towards his friend.

Elenna was already scrabbling to nock an arrow, but Tom could see she would be too slow.

"Get down!" he yelled. "Linka can't

risk grounding herself."

Elenna threw herself to the ground, belly first.

*Keeyaaaah!* Linka swooped low, her curved beak almost brushing Elenna's hair, then wheeled away again, swooping around for another pass.

Tom crouched low and edged his way towards his friend.

"What now?" Elenna said. "We can't fight lying down."

"I have an idea," Tom said. "But it'll need your rope, and your bow. We have to anchor her down."

"Good thinking." Elenna untied the rope from about her waist, and handed one end to Tom. The other end she knotted to an arrow shaft.

Tom took his end of the rope, and crawled towards a large boulder. Linka's shadow flitted across him, and Tom ducked as her great beak snapped at the air above his head. Linka screamed in frustration as she surged upwards and away. Tom wound the rope about the rock, pulling it tightly into cracks and crevices. Once it was secure, he nodded to Elenna.

Elenna stood and raised her bow as Linka swooped again. Linka's great eyes seemed to flash with triumph. She tipped her wings, and dived.

Elenna stood as still as a statue, staring down her arrow at the Beast. Linka hurtled on. Tom could barely watch. *She's leaving it too late!*

Elenna let the shaft fly, and dived towards the ground.

Linka surged past in a flurry of tawny feathers. Tom's coil of rope rippled into the air behind her.

*Twang!* The rope went taut. Elenna's barbed arrow was stuck fast in Linka's wing! Linka jerked towards the ground as the weight of the boulder wrenched her down.

The Beast screeched in panic, her eyes blazing with fury. She thrashed and strained, twisting and diving through the sky.

Beside Tom, Elenna put another arrow to her bowstring.

"No," Tom said. "We can't risk killing her. Defeating her is enough. Look, she's tiring."

Linka was tangled in the rope. One wing was partly bound to her body, and the rope was wrapped about her throat. Each time Linka twisted she became even more entwined. Each time she dived, she was reeled in closer to the ground. She twisted her beak to try and tear the arrow free, but she couldn't reach.

*All we have to do is wait...*

Linka swooped again, very low now. She still had Tom's dangling lasso tied about her neck. Tom sprang to his feet and lunged for it. His fingers closed on the rope and he braced his feet against the ground. Elenna was beside him in a flash, her hands next to his on the lasso.

Tom was almost tugged from his feet as the rope ran through his hands. He and Elenna stumbled forwards, half running, half falling, dragged across the mountaintop by the giant Beast.

There was a boulder just ahead. Tom angled towards it and wedged his feet against the stone.

"Hold on!" Tom gasped in agony. The pain in his palms was hard to bear, but he couldn't let go now. Not when they were so close. Side by side, the pair of them tugged.

A strangled cry erupted from Linka's beak as she strained against the ropes. Her head was raised and her breast thrust skyward as she beat her mighty wings.

"Pull!" cried Tom, and he and Elenna heaved. The rope bit into Tom's fingers and his arms shook as they dragged the giant bird downwards, closer to the ground.

Linka glared down at Tom, her eyes full of angry pride.

"Yield!" Tom yelled.

Linka gave a furious, drawn-out screech. Her eyes flashed defiantly. But then Tom felt the rope slacken.

"Pull!" Elenna grunted. "She's tiring."

Linka's wing-beats were slowing. Between each mighty thrust, Tom felt the rope in his hands grow slack. He looked at Elenna, and started to count.

"One…two…" Elenna held Tom's eye and nodded. "Three!" They both yanked the rope with all their might.

Linka jerked towards the ground
and crashed into the mountain.

The landing was all wrong. With
no legs, Linka couldn't steady herself.
Her feathers crumpled and her
wings bent. Tom winced as the bird's
pointed beak smashed into the stone.
Finally, Linka lay still, her wings

outspread and her giant head resting on the rocks.

Tom stepped out from behind the boulder and strode towards the Beast. He pulled his sword free from its sheath as he held her fiery gaze.

"Leave this place," Tom said. "You are vanquished."

The orange light in Linka's eyes seemed to flicker and fade. Thin lids came upwards to cover the glassy orbs. Linka lay quiet, her eyes closed and her breathing slow.

Then, quick as a kindled flame, Linka's eyes shot open.

*Whoosh!* Her snake-like tail flickered through the air, the glistening sting jabbing for Tom's face. Tom's arm came up quicker than he could think.

Linka's sting crashed against his shield. Tom swung his sword, smashing her tail aside with the flat of his blade. Then he smiled grimly at the Beast. "You've lost, Sky Conqueror," he said.

Linka gazed at Tom with a half-lidded, haughty stare. She ruffled her tawny feathers and, with an almost careless shrug, slowly started to fade. Soon only the shadow of one of her eyes remained, like the sun in a winter sky. Then that, too, was gone.

Tom let out a long shaky breath. All that was left of Linka was a single tawny feather, along with Slivka's scale. Tom put them into his bag.

Elenna came to his side. "One step closer to Master of the Beasts," she said. "But you really had me worried this time. You look terrible!"

Tom glanced down at himself. His tunic was torn and his hands and arms were grazed and bloody.

He smiled weakly. "Now all we have to do is rescue Aldo."

"Well, I think I've found some Stoneglass," Elenna said. She bent and picked up a lump of shiny blue-black stone. Where the light hit it, a dark rainbow of colour shimmered in its depths. "It is pretty," Elenna said. She tucked it into her tunic.

Tom flexed his aching foot, then looked out across the mountains towards Pyrus. "If only getting down could be as easy..." he said.

# CHAPTER TEN

# THE FINAL CHOICE

Silver lifted his head and sniffed the air.

"Can you smell dinner?" Elenna asked. "I think we're almost back." Silver wagged his tail.

Before long, Tom caught the tang of wood smoke on the breeze and the smell of roasting meat. He could see the welcoming lights of Pyrus flickering ahead. Tom thought of

Asha, waiting in the village, and glanced at Aldo beside him. The boy had been a real help on the long climb down Sunspear, finding paths that Tom and Elenna might have missed.

"I can't wait to see Asha!" Aldo said as they passed the first of the huts. "She'll be so relieved. I bet she thought I was dead..." A bent figure stood silhouetted in a doorway nearby. "Hey!" Aldo broke into a run. "Asha! It's me!"

"Aldo!" Asha hobbled towards her brother, dropping her crutches as he caught her up in a hug. "I thought I'd never see you again!"

Aldo stooped to pick up his sister's crutches, then took her arm. "It's thanks to Tom and Elenna that I'm still alive," he said.

Asha's eyes shone in the darkness.
"Thank you," she said. "For all you've
done."

Together, they headed into the
village.

Tom and Elenna found Petra sitting
beside a roaring fire outside Oran's

111

hut. She was drinking from a goblet, staring into the flames.

"Well, well, well," she said, looking up as they approached. "I'm surprised. Very unexpected." Petra took another sip from her cup. "You have my Stoneglass?"

Elenna put her hand inside her cloak and drew out several pieces of the dark stone. They glistened in the firelight, a thousand colours flickering across their surfaces. Petra's hand darted forwards, but Elenna snatched the Stoneglass away.

Tom held Petra's gaze. "You said you would show me the Road," he said.

Petra chuckled and drew herself up a little. "Did I?" she asked, watching Tom through her lashes.

He could feel his temper rising and

put his hand on his sword.

"Very well," Petra said at last. She turned to Elenna. "Throw one of the pieces in the fire."

Elenna raised an eyebrow at Tom. Tom nodded. Elenna stepped forwards and let a dark, shimmering rock fall from her hand into the flames. The fire crackled and hissed, sending up a shower of purple sparks, then died down to a pale blue flame. The inky surface of the Stoneglass smoothed and spread as the rock slowly melted, forming a flat, dark sheet.

Petra took a set of silver tongs from her robe, and carefully removed the slab. She blew lightly on the surface, then tipped the water from her goblet onto the stone. A hiss of steam enveloped Petra's features, and when the cloud cleared, she was holding

the sheet of Stoneglass out towards
Tom.

"Take it," Petra said. "It's my side of
the bargain."

Tom took the sheet. It was still
warm from the fire, and felt curiously
light and very smooth. Blues, greens
and silvers played across its surface,
along with flickers of red and gold.
But it was pretty. Nothing more. Tom
narrowed his eyes.

"I need to find the Road," he said
grimly.

"Look through it," Petra said. Tom
lifted the sheet to his eyes, and stared
into the flames. The world appeared
slightly dimmer, but otherwise
unchanged.

"I can't see—"

"Now turn around," Petra said. Tom
turned, and gasped. A narrow track of

red light ran right through the village out into the mountains and beyond. Tom felt a surge of hope.

"The Warrior's Road!" he said.

Elenna reached to take the Stoneglass tablet from him. She held it to her eyes. "Now I can see it, too!" she said. She turned back to Tom. "Now let's go and get some of that food I can smell. I'm starving."

Silver's ears pricked up.

"Good idea!" said Tom.

Next morning, Tom stood with his back to the village, looking through his Stoneglass tablet and out at the Warrior's Road. The cool morning air felt good against his skin, and a huge meal and a good rest had gone a long way to restoring his energy.

Elenna and Silver were close beside him, and Petra had come to see them off. The sky was still half dark, but an ominous red glow tinged the clouds above the mountains.

"Time to go," Tom said. He lowered the Stoneglass, which he had tied about his neck with a leather cord, and turned to Petra. "What will you do now?" he asked.

"Oh, I don't know." Petra shrugged. "I'm in no rush to be away. Being treated like royalty rather suits me."

"Come on," Elenna said. "We'd better go before the villagers are up."

The flickering red trail led Tom, Elenna and Silver up and down rocky, winding paths towards a distant range of mountains. Each time a new landscape opened up before them, Tom checked his Stoneglass to keep them on the right track.

Before long, they hit a cold, dense pocket of fog. It clung to Tom's skin and swirled about him, chilling him to the bone.

"We'd never be able to follow the Road in the fog without the Stoneglass," Tom said. "Maybe Petra's not all bad."

"Hmmm..." Elenna kicked a rock out of her way. "Just because she helped us when it paid her doesn't mean she won't lead us right into one of the Judge's traps."

"You're probably right," Tom said. "I wonder if—"

"Look out!" Elenna grabbed Tom's shoulder and Silver snarled into the mist. Tom looked down. The gravel and stone of the mountain pass they were following stopped at his feet, plunging into swirling mist. They were standing at the edge of what seemed like a bottomless crevasse.

Tom lifted his Stoneglass. Sure enough, the flickering ribbon of light that marked the Warrior's Road stopped dead about a foot ahead, hanging in the air.

"This must be like that icy pool," Tom said. "Time for another leap of faith."

"Off there?" Elenna said. "If you're wrong, we'll get more than a cold bath this time."

"She's right, boy." The gravelly voice came from behind them. Tom turned, and locked eyes with the Hooded Man.

"You!" Tom said. He drew his sword.

The man raised his hands and

gazed at Tom from under his hood.
"I'm not here to fight you this time,"
he said. "I'm here to give you some
advice. Give up. Turn back while you

still can. You're not made of strong enough steel to face the Warrior's Road. It will break you."

Tom felt his fist tighten on his sword. *How dare you!*

"Only time will tell if I am strong enough," Tom said. "As long as Avantia needs me, and while there's blood in my veins, I mean to follow the Road."

"Fool!" the man growled. "Nothing lies below except your untimely death."

Tom drove his sword hard into its scabbard.

"I wasn't sure I was going to jump," he said, "but your advice has made up my mind. You tried to kill me back in that cave. Nothing you say can be trusted!" Tom turned to Elenna. "Are you ready?" he asked.

Elenna nodded firmly. "Ready," she said.

Tom smiled. His Quest awaited him.

With a single step, he walked backwards over the edge of the cliff and plunged into the swirling mists of the abyss.

Join Tom on the next stage
of the Beast Quest, when he faces

# VERMOK
## THE SPITEFUL SCAVENGER!

## Series 13: THE WARRIOR'S ROAD
## COLLECT THEM ALL!

The Warrior's Road is Tom's toughest challenge yet. Will he succeed where so many have failed?

978 1 40832 402 8

978 1 40832 403 5

978 1 40832 404 2

978 1 40832 405 9

978 1 40832 406 6

978 1 40832 407 3

# Win an exclusive
# Beast Quest T-shirt and goody bag!

In every Beast Quest book the Beast Quest logo is
hidden in one of the pictures. Find the logos in books
73 to 78 and make a note of which pages they appear
on. Write the six page numbers on a postcard and
send it in to us.
Each month we will draw one winner to receive
a Beast Quest T-shirt and goody bag.

THE BEAST QUEST COMPETITION:
The Warrior's Road
Orchard Books
338 Euston Road, London NW1 3BH
Australian readers should email:
childrens.books@hachette.com.au

New Zealand readers should write to:
Beast Quest Competition
4 Whetu Place, Mairangi Bay, Auckland, NZ
or email: childrensbooks@hachette.co.nz

Only one entry per child.
Final draw: January 2014

You can also enter this competition
via the Beast Quest website: www.beastquest.co.uk

# Join the Quest,
# Join the Tribe

# www.beastquest.co.uk

Have you checked out the Beast Quest website?
It's the place to go for games, downloads, activities,
sneak previews and lots of fun!

You can read all about your favourite Beasts,
download free screensavers and desktop wallpapers
for your computer, and even challenge your friends
to a Beast Tournament.

Sign up to the newsletter at www.beastquest.co.uk
to receive exclusive extra content and the
opportunity to enter special members-only
competitions. We'll send you up-to-date info on all
the Beast Quest books, including the next exciting
series which features four brand-new Beasts!

Get 30% off all Beast Quest Books at www.beastquest.co.uk
Enter the code BEAST at the checkout.